Friends

Phidal

Barbie's BFFs

Barbie's fab life wouldn't be the same without her best friends. Match your stickers to the shadows so you can see who they are.

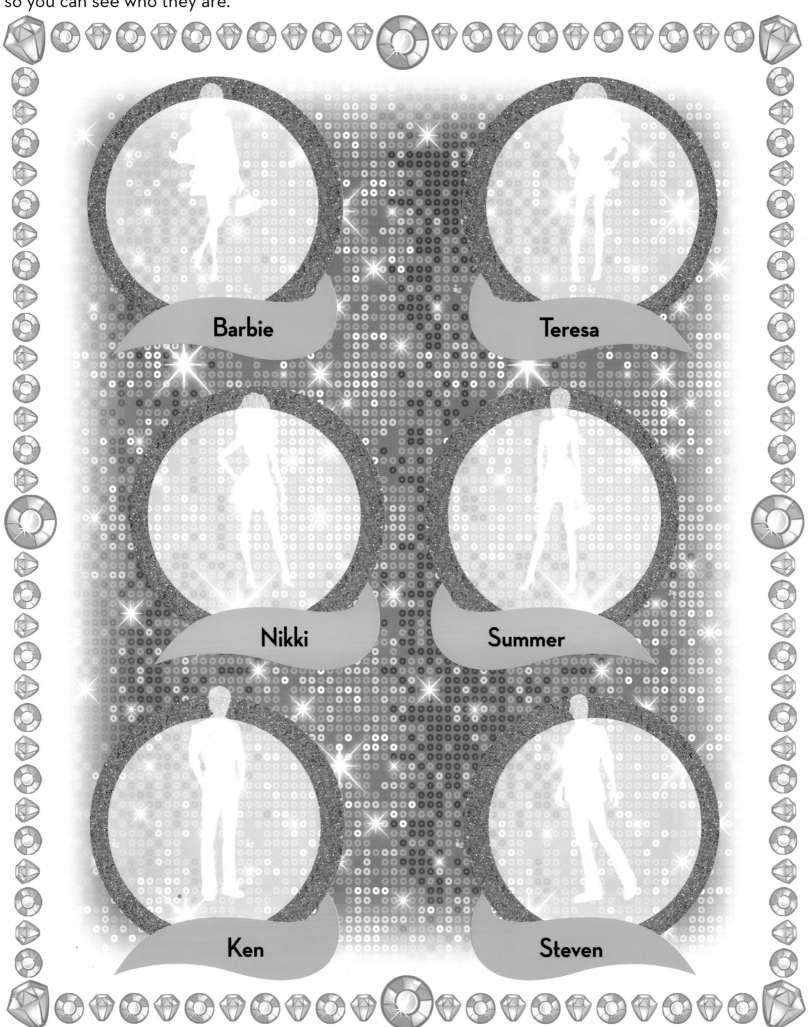

Barbie

Teresa

Nikki

Summer

Ken

Steven

I Love...

It's great to be passionate about things! Match your stickers to the shadows to find out what Barbie and her friends love.

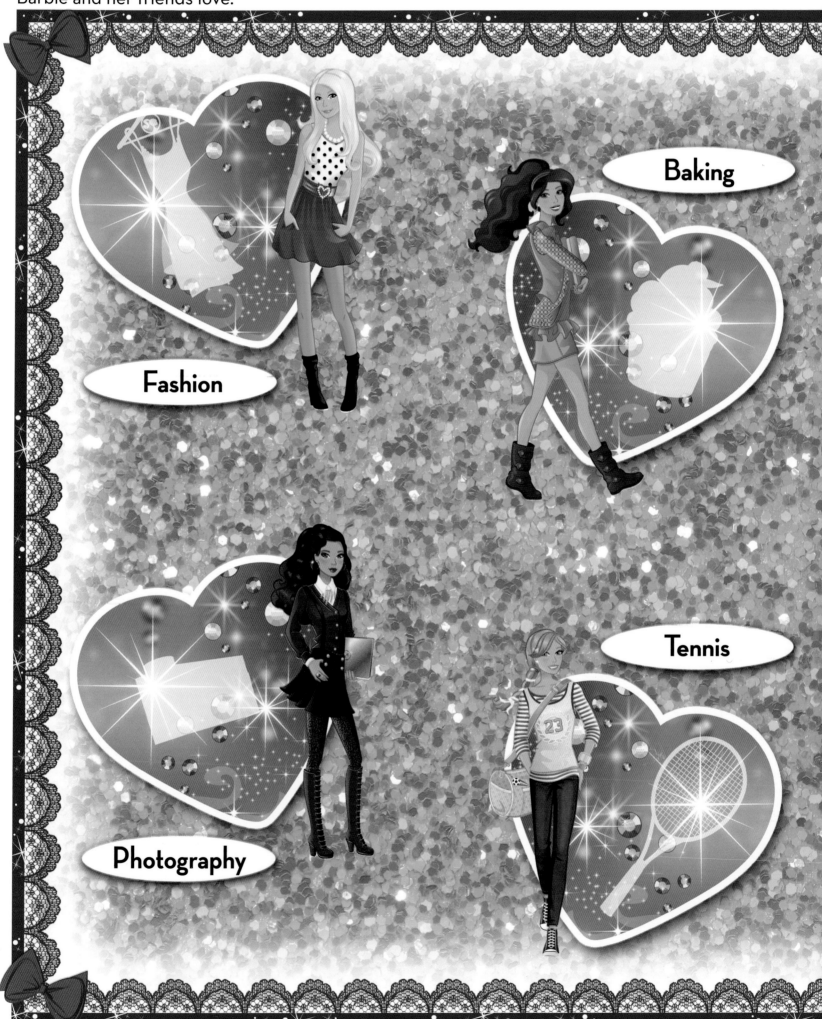

Fashion

Baking

Photography

Tennis

Pool Party!

When the gang is not working on amazing projects, they're having fun by Barbie's pool.
Use your stickers to get this pool party started!

Fave Spots

Barbie and her friends each have places they love to be. Use your stickers to find out who likes to hang out in each of these spots.

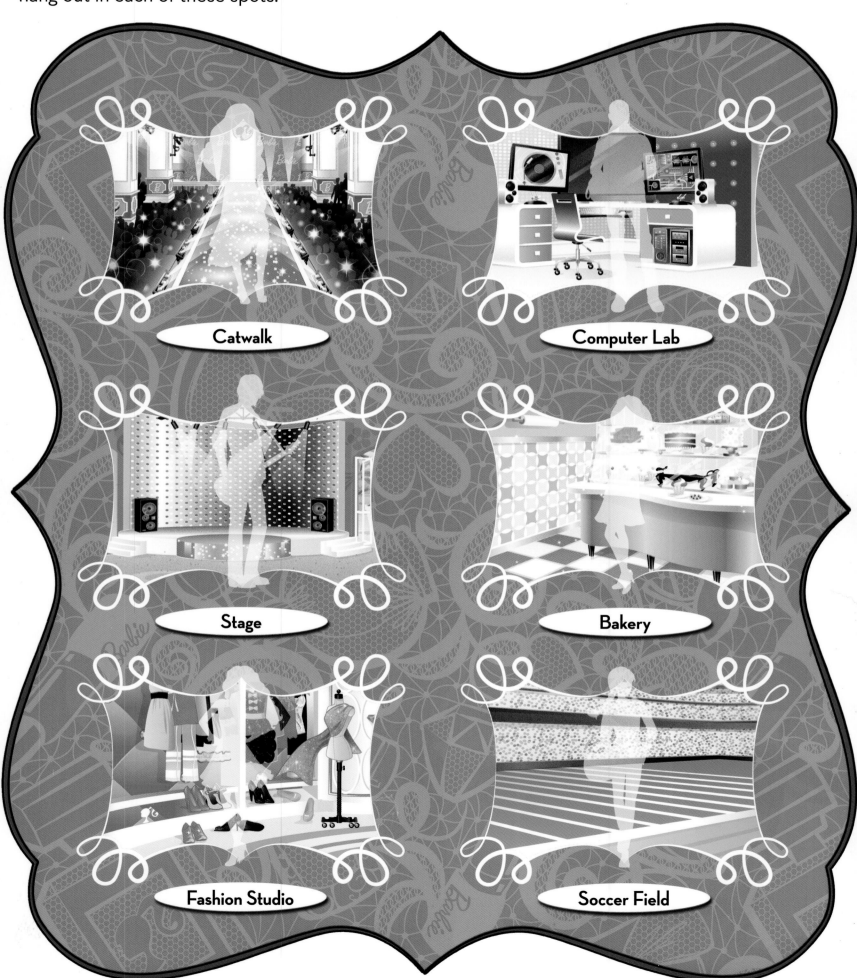

Catwalk

Computer Lab

Stage

Bakery

Fashion Studio

Soccer Field

Familiar Faces

These teens not only have unique personalities, but also unique looks. Can you figure out who is who? Match your stickers to the shadows.

Picture Perfect

Barbie, Teresa, and Nikki are hanging out in the living room. Use your stickers to complete the scene.

Garden Guests

Everything is set for Barbie's garden party... but where is everyone? Use your stickers to make the bottom scene look like the top one!

Sisters

Phidal

Big Sister

Meet the best big sis ever! Skipper, Stacie, and Chelsea adore Barbie. Use your stickers to match Barbie's little sisters to their shadows.

Skipper

Stacie

Chelsea

Thumbs Up!

Although the sisters have lots in common, they are each unique and are each interested in different things. Use your stickers to find out what they like.

Everyone's Welcome!

The girls love spending time together at home. Nothing beats a get-together with family and friends! Decorate the scene with your stickers.

12

13

14 15

16

Go Chelsea!

Chelsea, the youngest of the sisters, is a ball of energy! Match your stickers to the shadows to see what Chelsea is up to.

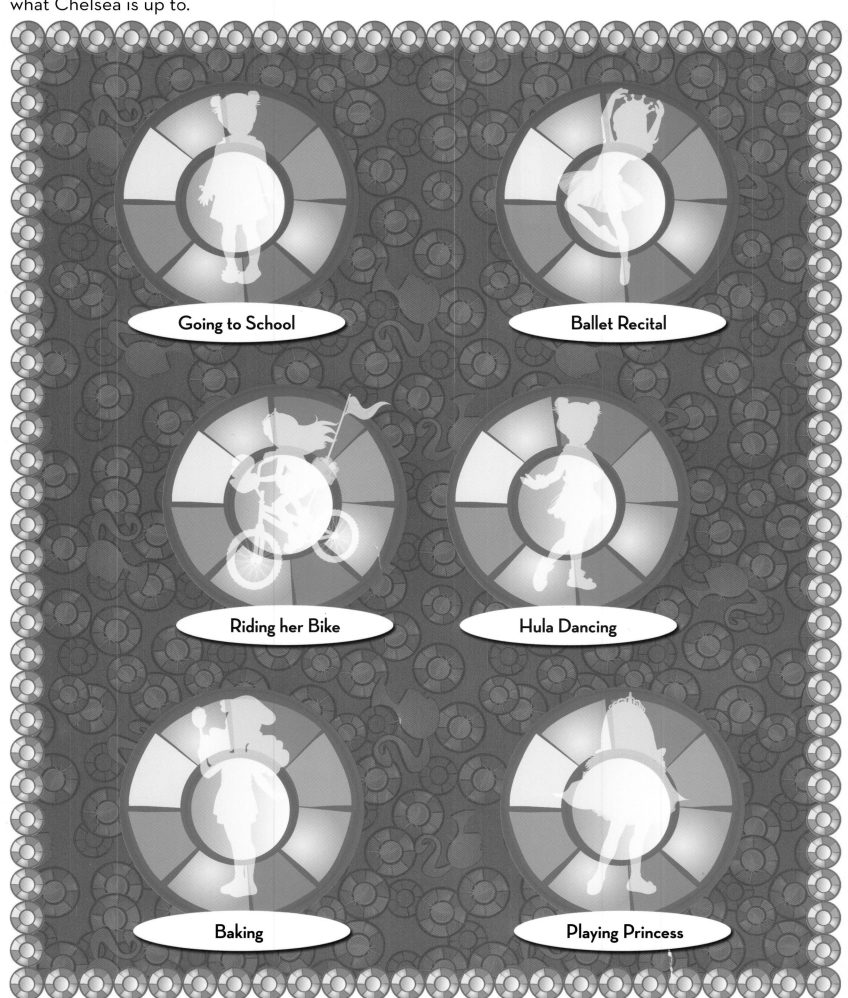

Going to School

Ballet Recital

Riding her Bike

Hula Dancing

Baking

Playing Princess

Special Spaces

Barbie is visiting her little sisters in their bedrooms. Use your stickers to match each sister to her bedroom.

Chelsea's Room

Stacie's Room

Skipper's Room

13

Slumber Party!

The sisters love having slumber parties together! Fill in the missing parts of the scene with your stickers.

Hanging Out

Even with their busy schedules, Barbie and her sisters are always finding time to hang out together. Use your stickers to make the bottom scene look like the top one.

Careers

P Phidal

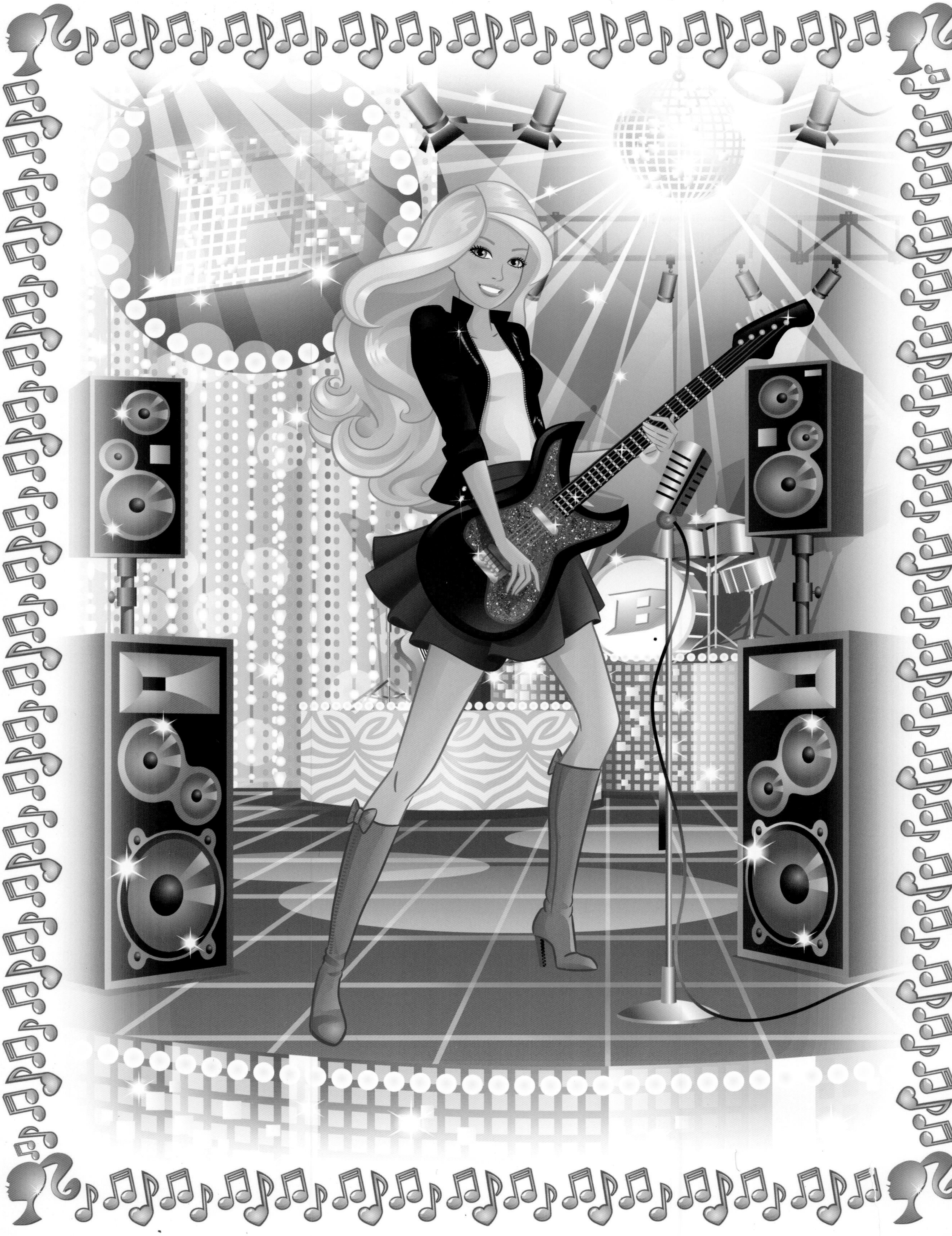

I Can Be... Anything!

Barbie has had many different careers. Match your stickers to the shadows to find out what they are.

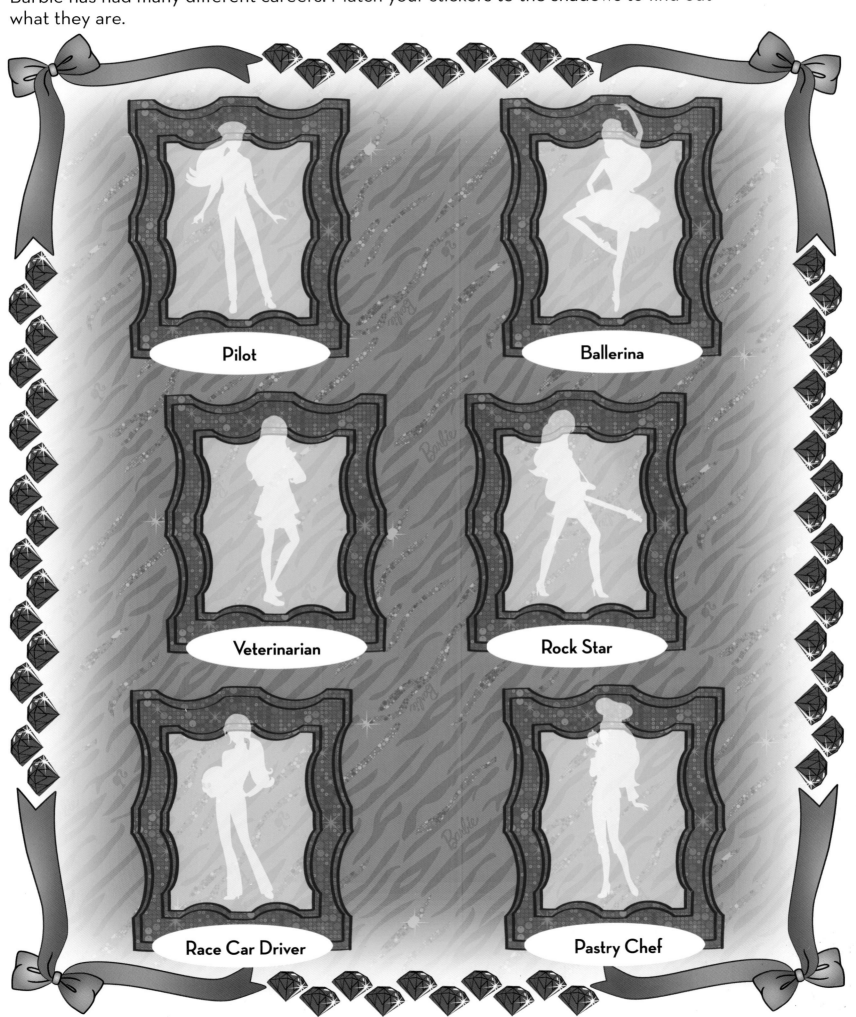

Pilot

Ballerina

Veterinarian

Rock Star

Race Car Driver

Pastry Chef

Tools of the Trade

All jobs come with their own set of accessories! Match your stickers to the shadows to see which objects go with each job.

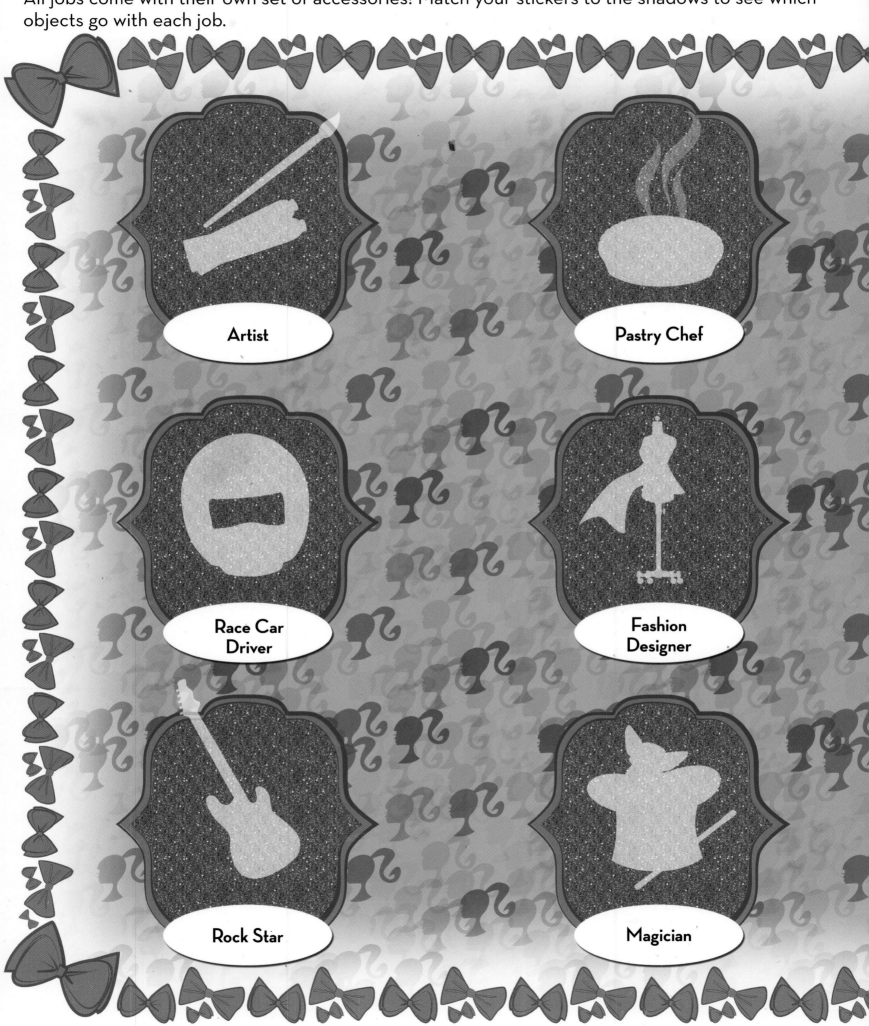

Artist

Pastry Chef

Race Car Driver

Fashion Designer

Rock Star

Magician

Actress

Paleontologist

Soccer Player

Astronaut

Teacher

Doctor

Barbie's Dream Closet

Wearing the right clothes for a job is important, and Barbie certainly has a lot to choose from! Use your stickers to decorate the scene.

Pet Doctor

Barbie is very good at taking care of animals. She's a natural-born veterinarian! Use your stickers to see all the animals she has examined.

Star Photographer

Sometimes Barbie likes to be behind the camera instead of in front of it! Match your stickers to the shadows to see some of the pictures she has taken.

Career Challenge

Always up for a challenge, Barbie has tried her hand at many things. Fill in the missing parts of each picture with your stickers.

When I Grow Up...

It's Career Day at Barbie's high school! What a great way to learn about different jobs! Use your stickers to make the bottom scene look like the top one.

Pets

P Phidal

Precious Pets

Barbie loves taking care of and playing with her many animal friends. Match your stickers with the shadows to see all the animals.

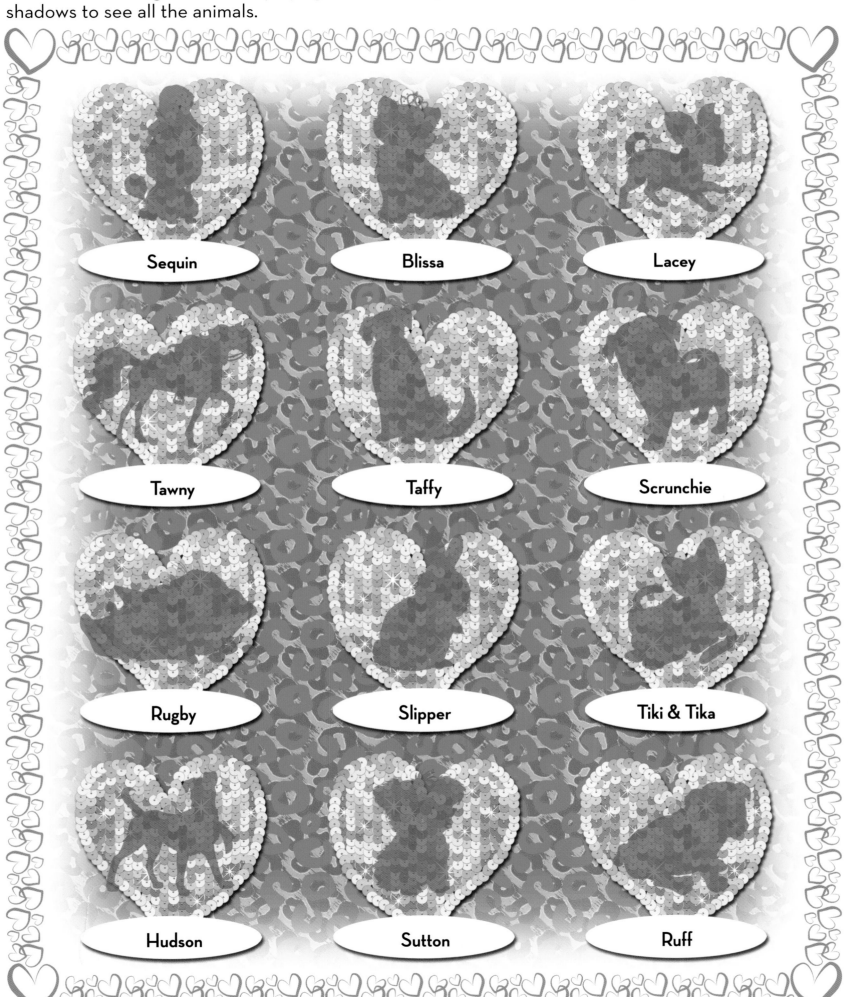

Sequin

Blissa

Lacey

Tawny

Taffy

Scrunchie

Rugby

Slipper

Tiki & Tika

Hudson

Sutton

Ruff

Four-legged Friends

Each of the pets has a human companion. Match your stickers to the shadows to make the perfect pairs.

Pet Meet!

Barbie and the gang enjoy taking their pets down to the waterfront for playtime. Use your stickers to bring this scene to life.

Snack Time

All the pets have foods they like best—or at least things they like to chew on! Use your stickers to reveal each pet's preference.

Stylish Pets

Just like Barbie and her friends, these pets like to look their best. Match your stickers to the shadows to see their favorite accessories.

Frolicking Friends

The girls and their pets are having a terrific time playing on the waterfront! Use your stickers to complete the image.

Red Carpet

Sequin, Lacey, and Blissa are making a red carpet appearance with the girls. Use your stickers to make the bottom scene look like the top one.

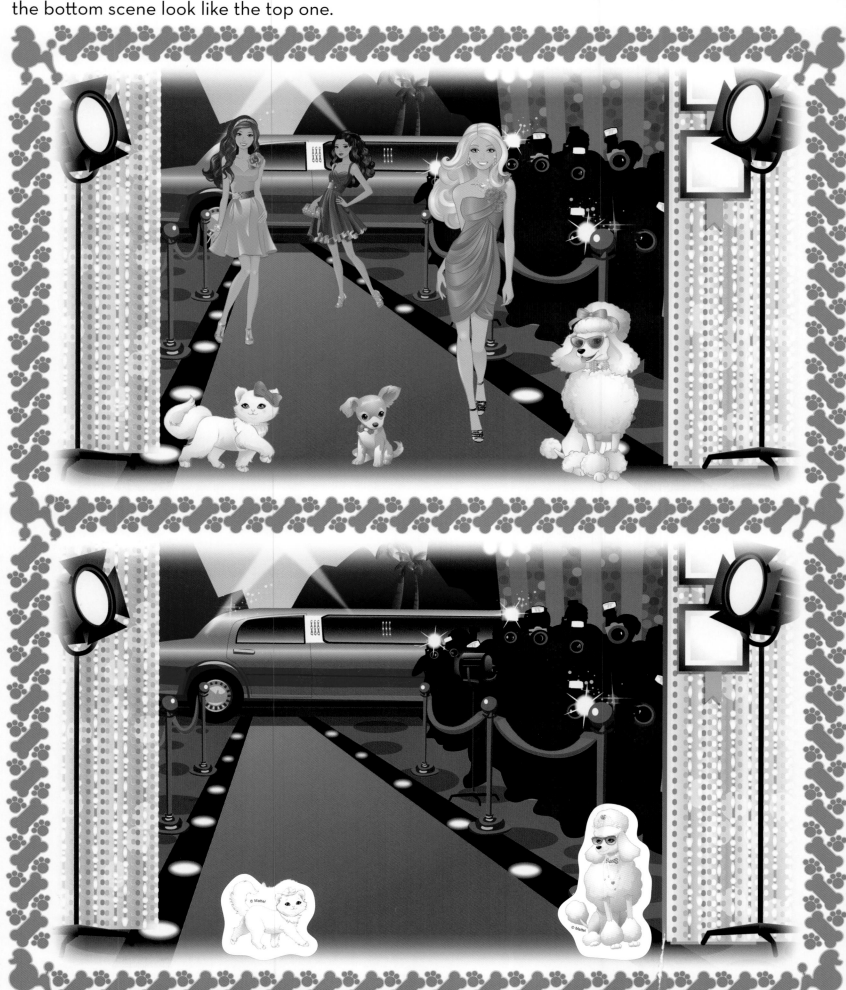

Fashion

Phidal

Fashion Sense

Barbie, Teresa, Nikki, and Raquelle love looking their best! Use your stickers to help them get ready.

Dress

Shoes

Purse

Jewelry

Nail Polish

Perfume

Stylish Designs

Barbie and the gang are always eager to wear the season's latest designs. Match your stickers to the shadows to see each friend's outfit.

Fashion Soirée

Barbie and her friends are strutting their stuff on the catwalk. Use your stickers to fill in the fashion show scene.

Fabulous Footwear

No outfit is complete without the right footwear! Match your stickers to the shadows to get a closer look at the shoes or boots each girl is wearing.

The Right Look

Barbie loves picking out the perfect thing to wear! Match your stickers to the shadows to help her get ready! Which outfit do you like the best?

What to Wear?

Barbie has just the right outfit for every occasion. Match your stickers to the shadows to see what she wears for each of the different situations.

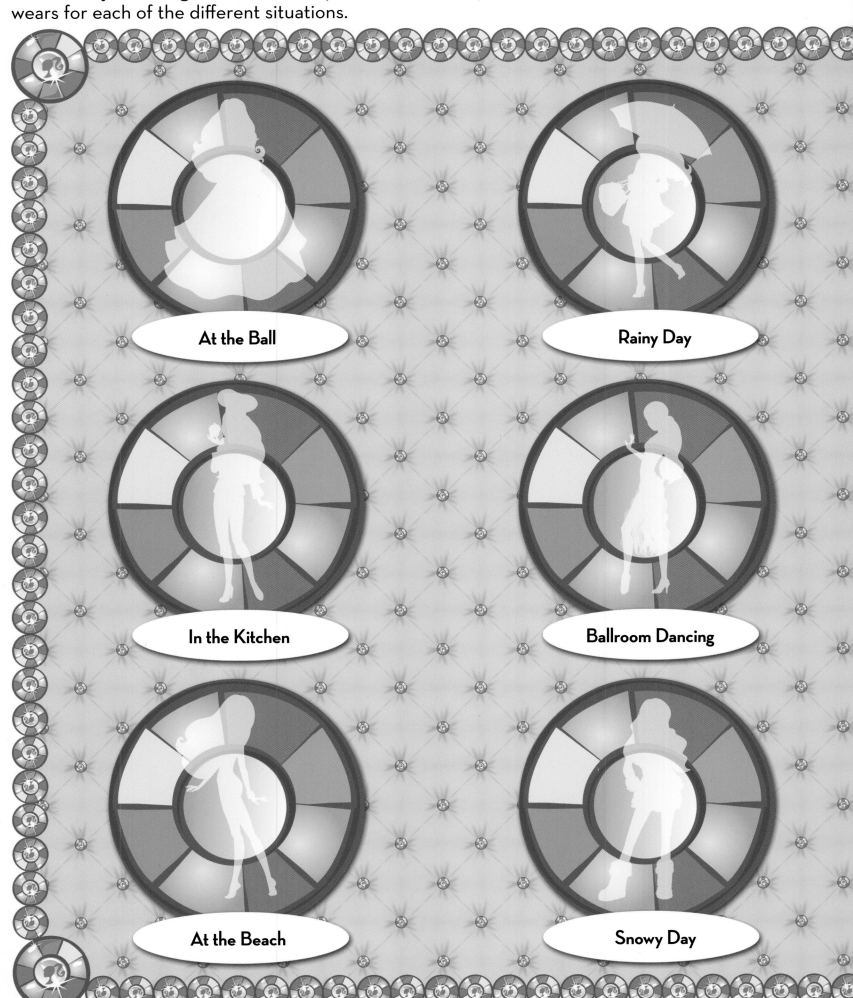

At the Ball

Rainy Day

In the Kitchen

Ballroom Dancing

At the Beach

Snowy Day

Rocking Out

Playing Tennis

Doing Yoga

Garden Party

At School

Sleepover

No Ordinary Closet!

Barbie's walk-in closet is filled with fabulous clothes, footwear, and accessories. Use your stickers to make the bottom scene look like the top one.

Sports

Phidal

Go Barbie!

Barbie loves to be active. Match your stickers to the shadows to see what sports and activities she does.

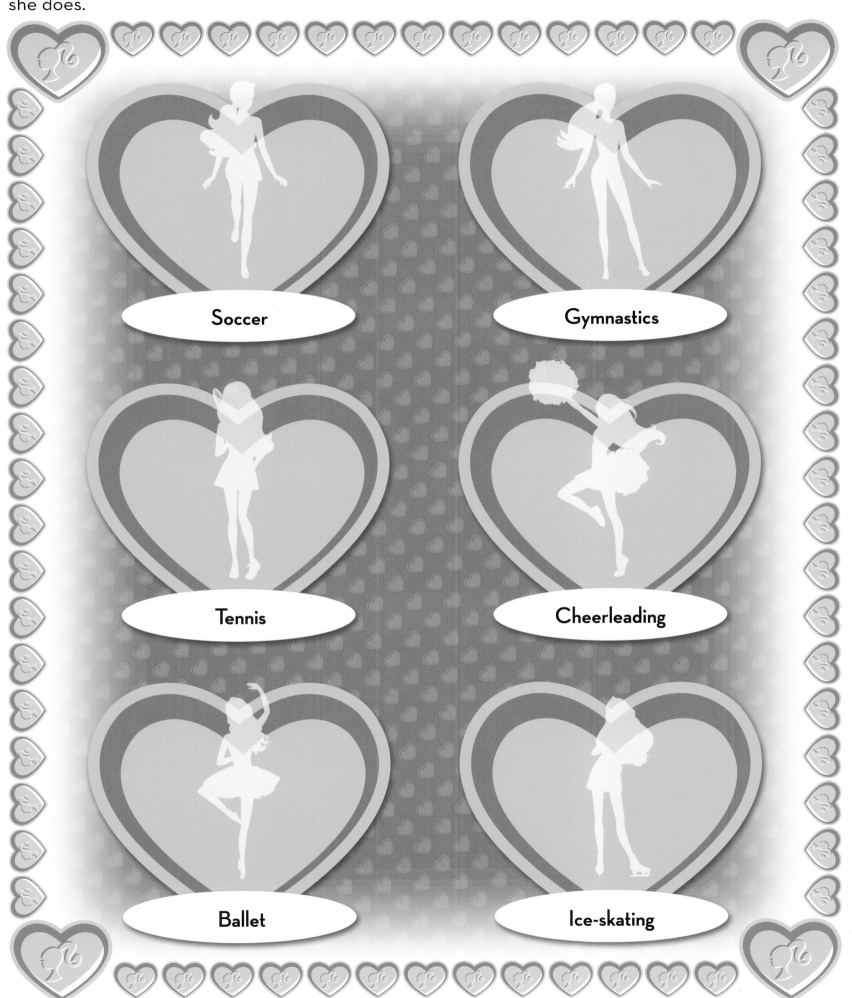

Soccer

Gymnastics

Tennis

Cheerleading

Ballet

Ice-skating

The Right Stuff

Many sports require special equipment. Match your stickers to the shadows to see what's needed for each sport.

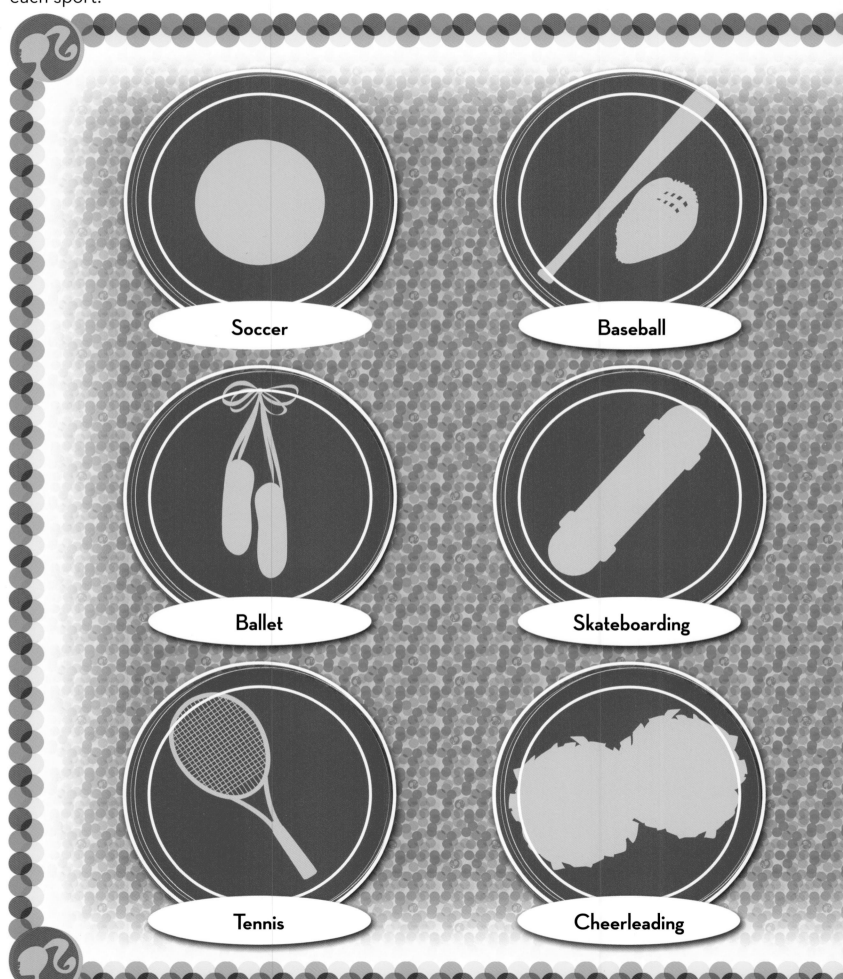

Soccer

Baseball

Ballet

Skateboarding

Tennis

Cheerleading

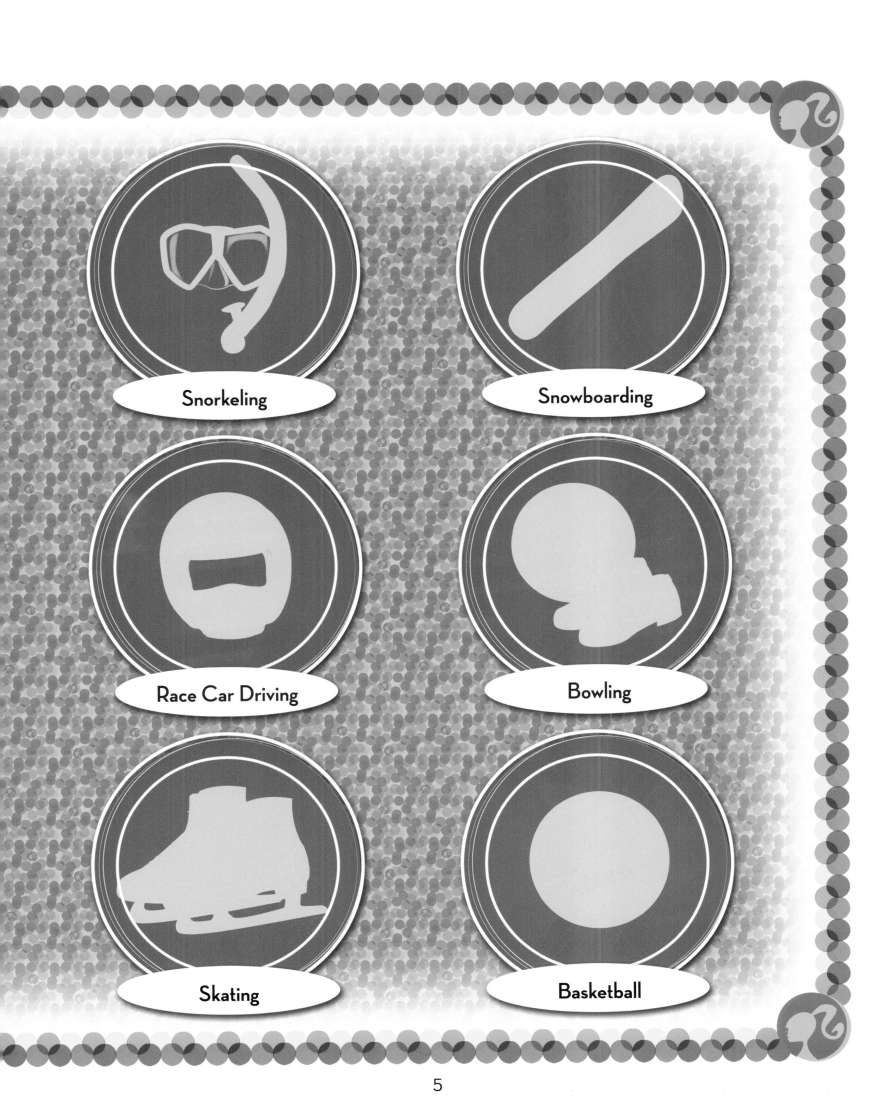

Snorkeling

Snowboarding

Race Car Driving

Bowling

Skating

Basketball

Soccer Match

The stadium is packed with excited fans. It's almost kickoff time! Bring this soccer field to life with your stickers.

Team Barbie!

Barbie is working on a fabulous new logo for her team. Help her finish it by decorating it with your stickers.

Skateboard Design

Barbie wants to customize her brand-new skateboard. Use your stickers to help her make it look fabulous.

Practice Makes Perfect

Barbie is great at lots of different sports. Match your stickers to the shadows to see what sports she is playing.

Swim-tastic

Barbie and the gang get lots of exercise swimming... but they also like to relax by the pool! Use your stickers to make the bottom scene look like the top one.